The Berenstain Bears
and the
HOMEWORK HASSLE

If you're a bear for TV,
loud music, and fun,
how ya gonna get
your homework done?

A First Time Book®

Dear Parent,
I regret to report that Brother Bear has fallen too far behind in his homework. Please call me.

Yours truly,
Teacher Bob

The Berenstain Bears
and the
HOMEWORK HASSLE

Stan & Jan Berenstain

Random House 🏠 New York

Copyright © 1997 by Berenstain Enterprises, Inc. All rights reserved under International and Pan-American Copyright Conventions.
Published in the United States by Random House, Inc., New York, and simultaneously in Canada by Random House of Canada Limited, Toronto.   http://www.randomhouse.com/
Library of Congress Cataloging-in-Publication Data: Berenstain, Stan, 1923-   The Berenstain Bears and the homework hassle / Stan & Jan Berenstain.   p.   cm. — (First time books)
SUMMARY: Brother gets in trouble when he allows television, his boom box, the telephone, and other distractions to keep him from doing his homework.
ISBN 0-679-88744-X (trade) — 0-679-98744-4 (lib. bdg.) [1. Homework—Fiction. 2. Bears—Fiction.] I. Berenstain, Jan, 1923- II. Title.
III. Series: Berenstain, Stan, 1923- First time books. PZ7.B4483Beffi 1997 [E]—dc21 97-6753 Printed in the United States of America 10 9 8 7 6 5 4 3 2 1

Mama was sitting in her favorite chair straightening up her sewing basket when she sniffed the air and said, "What's that funny smell?"

Papa looked up from the evening paper and sampled the air. "Hmmm," he said. "I smell it, too. It smells like…"

"Garbage!" said Mama. "It smells like garbage."

Papa sniffed again. "Now, where do you suppose…"

"I'll tell you where I suppose!" said Mama, who had put aside her sewing basket and sniffed around the room. "It's coming from Brother's backpack."

And sure enough, it was. There was an old banana peel, a brown apple core, and a moldy piece of bread in Brother's backpack.

But that wasn't all there was in Brother's backpack. Among the books and papers was a letter. It was old and wrinkled, and it was from his teacher. Mama read it.

Then she passed it to Papa. After Papa read it, he looked across the table at Brother, who was doing his homework.

At least, he was *supposed* to be doing his homework. And maybe he was. But it was hard to tell by looking at him. He had a card table set up in front of the television, that was showing his favorite program, *The Bear Stooges*. He was listening to his boom box and talking into a cell phone at the same time. There was a Game Bear and a bowl of popcorn on the TV. And, oh yes, there were some school books and a paper and pencil, too.

"Excuse me, young sir," said Papa. "Is this the Mars space station?"

"I'll get back to you, Fred," said Brother.

He put down the cell phone and turned off the boom box. "I'm not quite reading you, Dad."

"You're not reading much of anything, according to this letter from your teacher. You may as well have *been* on Mars for all the attention you've been paying to your homework lately," said Papa.

"Letter? What letter?" asked Brother.

"This old, wrinkled letter that Mama found in your backpack," said Papa. The letter may have been old and wrinkled, but its message was clear.

Dear Parent
I regret to report that Brother Bear has fallen too far behind in his homework. Please call me.

Yours truly
Teacher Bob

"In my backpack?" said Brother. "I thought my backpack was private."

"When something starts to smell like garbage," said Mama, "it isn't private anymore."

Sister Bear couldn't resist putting her two cents in. "I don't see how you expect Brother to keep up with his homework. He has so many more *interesting* things to do. There's soccer, basketball, video games, going around like a big shot, and *girls*."

Brother turned on Sister. "Why, you little…!"

"That will be quite enough, Sister," said Papa. "Why don't you go do your own homework?"

"It's all done," said Sister. "See?"

"You call those scribbles homework, you little twerp?" shouted Brother.

"Now," said Mama, "let's everyone calm down and try to figure out what the problem is."

"I'll tell you what the problem is! The problem is too much homework! Vocabulary homework! Arithmetic homework! Science homework! It's homework, homework, homework! Every subject! Every day till it's coming out of my ears!"

"Uh-huh," said Papa. "Tell me, son, what is your homework for today?"

"Adding and subtracting fractions and memorizing two stanzas of 'The Bear Stood on the Burning Deck.'"

"That really doesn't seem like too much homework to me, son," said Papa.

Brother slumped and stared at the Bear Stooges, who were busy hitting one another on the head.

"I'm not hearing any sort of explanation," said Papa. "I guess that's because tonight's homework isn't really the problem. The problem is that you haven't been handing in your homework on a daily basis. You haven't been taking care of business. You've been falling behind."

"Gee, what's going to happen?" asked Brother as the living room phone rang.

"It's the BRS," said Mama. "For you, Papa."

"Take their number and I'll call them back," said Papa.

"What's the BRS, Mama?" asked Sister.

"It's the Bears' Revenue Service," said Mama. "They collect taxes."

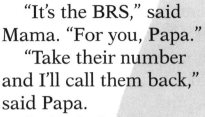

"What's going to happen," said Papa, "is that there's not going to be any more Mars space station. No more boom box. No more popcorn. It's just you and your homework until you're all caught up."

"But that'll take forever!" moaned Brother.
"Nevertheless," said Papa.

"You just don't understand!" said Brother, heading for the door.
"Where are you going?" asked Mama.

"I'm just going for a walk," said Brother.

As often happened when Brother had a problem and went for a walk, his feet led him to Gramps and Gran's, just down the road.

Gramps and Gran could tell Brother was in trouble as soon as they opened the door. After some milk and cookies, Brother told them the whole miserable story: the telltale letter, the missed assignments, the no television, the no video games, the no anything until he caught up. And he was so far behind that he'd never catch up.

"Oh, you'll catch up," said Gramps. "Your father did."

"Huh?" said Brother.

"Same thing happened with your dad when he was your age," said Gramps. "Of course, there was no television then."

No television, thought Brother. Wow! That would have been like *really* being on Mars!

"We had radio," continued Gramps. "We still have it, of course. But radio was like television then. It had great stories every evening. There was a Western called *Bearsmoke*, and *Buck Bruin in the Twenty-Fifth Century* was sort of like *Bear Trek* is now. And your dad listened to them while he did his homework. And he was big on sports, just as you are. So he fell further and further behind. I clamped down on him, just the way he's clamping down on you."

Gee, thought Brother. Papa *does* understand. The thought that he'd gone through it all himself made Brother feel a little bit better.

A stranger was meeting with Papa
when Brother got home.
"He's from the BRS," said Sister.
"It has something to do with taxes. It
looks like Papa hasn't been taking
care of business, either."

The stranger was about to leave.

"We'll be glad to give you a little more time. But you're going to have to catch up," he said as he left.

And that's how it worked out. Brother
sat on one side of the card table, and Papa
sat on the other side.
    It was a good lesson for both of them.